DILYS PRICE

NORMAN
PRICE

BELLA
LASAGNE

JAMES

SARAH

MEET ALL THESE FRIENDS IN BUZZ BOOKS:

Thomas the Tank Engine
Tiny Toon Adventures
Looney Tunes
Bugs Bunny
Fireman Sam
Joshua Jones
Toucan 'Tecs
Flintstones
Jetsons

First published 1991 by Buzz Books,
an imprint of Reed International Books Ltd
Michelin House, 81 Fulham Road, London SW3 6RB
Reprinted 1992

LONDON MELBOURNE AUCKLAND

Fireman Sam © 1985 Prism Art & Design Ltd

Text © 1991 William Heinemann Ltd
Illustrations © 1991 William Heinemann Ltd
Based on the animation series produced by Bumper Films
for S4C/Channel 4 Wales and Prism Art & Design Ltd.
Original idea by Dave Gingell and Dave Jones,
assisted by Mike Young. Characters created by Rob Lee.
All rights reserved.

ISBN 1 85591 110 8

Printed and bound in the UK by BPCC Hazell Books Ltd

A SPOT OF BOTHER

Story by Caroline Hill-Trevor
Developed from a storyline by Rob Lee
and a script by Nia Ceidiog

Illustrations by The County Studio

It was the last day of term and Sarah and
James were on their way to school.

"Hurry up, Norman," called James.
"It's the best day of term, remember?"

"Not for me," mumbled Norman. "I've
got to do the spelling test again."

6

"Hello you two, waiting for Norman as usual?" said Fireman Sam, who had come for his newspaper. "How about a treat for break time?"

"Oo, yes please, Uncle Sam," the twins replied.

"Well, I never," said Dilys. "There's a chicken-pox epidemic in Pontypandy valley. Newspaper for you, Fireman Sam?" She folded up the paper she had been reading and handed it over.

"Oh er, thanks," said Fireman Sam.

"I'll have two of those chocolate bars for Sarah and James as well, please," he said.

"Where's Norman?" asked Sarah. "He was here a moment ago."

"Won't be long. Just learning my spelling," Norman shouted from upstairs.

"Mam, I've got spots!" cried Norman, racing downstairs.

"Ooo, my poor darlin'," cried Dilys. "It's that chicken-pox. I knew it, he's so sensitive. Look at all those spots!"

"Don't worry, Mam. I'll go to bed after school," Norman coughed feebly.

"You'll go upstairs right this minute!" ordered Dilys.

"We'd better go before we all catch chicken-pox too," shrugged James, looking at his watch.

"Hope you feel better soon, Norman!" called Fireman Sam as they all left the shop.

Up at the fire station, Elvis was giving Trevor his breakfast.

"Why don't you try some muesli, Trevor?" asked Penny. "It's much healthier."

"Thanks, Penny, but my appetite's healthy enough already!" said Trevor tucking into bacon and eggs.

"Right, here are the duties for today,"
said Station Officer Steele. "Fireman Sam,
you're on call. Firefighter Morris, check
food supplies. Cridlington and Evans . . .
timed jogging. And no excuses!"

"But, Sir, lunch is just going into the oven
– it'll burn," Elvis pleaded.

Meanwhile, as soon as Dilys was busy,
Norman leaped out of bed and wiped his
'spots' off with a tissue. "I'm not wasting
the day indoors!" he said.

He'd reached Pandy Lane when he saw
two figures in the distance. They gave him
an idea.

14

"That's odd," said Elvis, looking at the
road sign and frowning. "I thought
Pontypandy was that way."

"Mmm, me too," Trevor agreed,
scratching his head.

Norman giggled as Trevor and Elvis took
the wrong turning.

15

"Let's stop here and wait for a bus," Elvis suggested when they came to a bus stop.

"It'll be a long wait, Elvis! I'm the bus driver, remember!" said Trevor. "But we may as well have a rest."

They sat down and fell fast asleep.

"Now for some real fun," Norman whispered. Being careful not wake them, he drew red spots on the sleeping firefighters' faces

"Glad I spotted you here! Hee hee!" he giggled to himself.

When Elvis and Trevor didn't come back, Fireman Sam and Station Officer Steele went to look for them.

"There they are, Sir," said Fireman Sam.

"Miles off course," muttered Station Officer Steele. "Whoever heard of a bus driver with no sense of direction!"

"Sir, they're covered in spots!" said Fireman Sam.

"In that case, they'll have to walk home. We can't risk infecting the whole force," Station Officer Steele said briskly.

Suddenly the alarm in Jupiter's cab sounded.

"Good heavens, there's a fire at the fire station," said Station Officer Steele, talking to Penny on the radio. "We need all hands to the pump for this one, spots or not. Into Jupiter everyone!"

  With the siren blaring and the lights
flashing, they raced through Pontypandy.
  "Mamma mia! It's the fire station – it's
burning down!" exclaimed Bella, pointing
at the cloud of smoke.

"Oh help! It's the gas cooker," said Elvis, going pale as he saw smoke pouring from the kitchen window.

"I thought jogging was a bad idea – first chicken-pox and now this," said Trevor. "Never again!"

"Well, don't just stand there, get the hose," yelled Station Officer Steele.

"I'll switch off the gas at the mains first," said Firefighter Penny Morris.

Fireman Sam and Firefighter Elvis Cridlingt
put on their air supply masks and picked up
the hose. Kicking open the door, they charg
into the smoke-filled kitchen.

"Stand by to help, this one looks serious,
Fireman Sam reported back over the radio.

"How's it going, Fireman Sam?" asked Station Officer Steele a few minutes later.

"Send reinforcements," came the reply.

"In you go, Firefighter Morris," ordered Station Officer Steele. Penny grabbed a fire extinguisher and went inside.

Inside the kitchen, the three of them soaked the cooker in a flood of water.

"Coming under control at last, Sir," said Fireman Sam, as the flames died down, leaving the scorched cooker smouldering.

"Well, I won't be cooking on that for a
it, I suppose," said Elvis wiping his face.
Phew, it's hot in here."

"Some good news anyway," grinned
ireman Sam. "Elvis, wipe your face again."

"Aw," exclaimed Elvis, "chicken-pox all
ver my fingers!"

Later that day, Fireman Sam was in Dilys's shop when Norman came skipping in.

"I'm better now, Mam," he said cheerfully.

"Norman Price, you get back into bed at once with all those spots!" said Dilys.

"You won't wipe those off so easily, my
boy," laughed Fireman Sam, as Norman
scrubbed frantically at his face.

"And Mrs Williams says you can do the
spelling test next term," said James.

"Mam," moaned Norman, "I feel ill!"

29

FIREMAN SAM

STATION OFFICER
STEELE

TREVOR EVANS

ELVIS
CRIDLINGTON

PENNY MORRIS